This book belongs to

....

5-minute enchanting tales

make
believe
ideas

CONTENTS

Mermaid Mia

and the Royal Visit

Lara Ede · Rosie Greening

Mermaid Mia loved to write new **stories** every day.

She ran the **paper** at her school with **Emily** and **Fay**.

Emily took the **photographs**...

Say cheese!

and Fay did the **reviews**.

The Mermail

But **Mia** was the one in charge of each day's **front-page** news.

8

Mia's news was **popular** and **always** told with style.

She was funny, frank, and honest, and her **words** made people smile.

One morning, **Mia** longed to find a juicy piece of **news.**

She got her **pad** and went in **search** of **something** she could use.

Her first lead was a story
on the **snails** in the canteen.

But the **news** was **SO** s-l-o-w–m-o-v-i-n-g, Mia **really** wasn't keen.

Then she heard a **rumor** of a **whale** stuck in the **gym**.

"Now **that's** a story," **Mia** thought. "I'll write my news on him!"

1, 2, 3, push!

But just as **Mia** reached the **whale**, he managed to get **out**.

"My front page will be bare!"
she cried.
"What can I write about?"

Suddenly, a sneaky thought **popped** into **Mia's** head.

"The **real** news isn't good enough –
I'll **make it up** instead!"

She **swam** back to the newsroom
and began to type full speed.

"This **news** will make a **splash**," she thought.
"They're **sure** to want to read!"

The Mermail

Queen Marina is one of the most popular royals under the sea. Whether it's recycling in the coral beds, or opening libraries, the queen always has a new project on the go.
Just last month, it was Queen Marina's birthday. It was a magical day, with tasty treats, a fantastic band, and comedy from the clown fish.

The biggest gift Queen Marina received was a beautiful carriage, though it has yet to be used out in public. We believe she is saving it for a special occasion...

As soon as it was printed,
Mia's words began to **spread,**

STARFISH ACADEMY

and the school **buzzed** with **excitement**
at the **front-page** news that said . . .

The Mermail

A ROYAL VISIT!

Written by Mermaid Mia

Queen Marina

The Royal Palace

Her Highness, Queen Marina will be visiting our school. She's heard of the academy and wants to meet us all!

It was all the **mermaids** talked about: the **best** news of the year! In class, they'd whisper **happily**:

"The **Queen** is coming **HERE!**"

I can't wait!

I bet we'll have a ball.

But soon the **news** got out of hand, which made poor **Mia** fret.
And as the day drew closer, she kept **hoping** they'd **forget**.

With one week left, she told her friends:

"I've made a **big mistake.**

The **queen's** not **really** visiting –

the news I wrote was **fake!**"

"You **should** have told the **truth**," said Fay.
"But now we need a **plan**.
We'll tell the queen what happened
and then **fix** this if we can."

So **Mia** sent a **letter**
to the queen's **royal** address.

She asked the queen to **help** them out,
and **hoped** that she'd say **yes**.

Soon the **royal whale mail** brought a very special note.

You've got mail!

Mermaid Mia
Starfish Academy
Under the Sea

It was signed "Love, **Queen Marina**,"
and this is what she wrote . . .

Dear Mia,

You're very brave for owning up —
it's not easy to do.
And thank you for inviting me,
I'd love to visit you!

Love,
Queen Marina

At last, the **special** day arrived;
the **mermaids** couldn't wait.

They lined the school with **pretty flags,** and a **sign** that said, "YOU'RE GREAT!"

A **carriage** pulled by **dolphins** soon drew up and parked outside.

She waved to me!

I love her crown.

The **queen** swam up to meet them all, and Mia **beamed** with **pride.**

The day was so **amazing**, Mia knew what she **should** do.

Miss Isabella meets Queen Marina

The queen's new fitness plan is a slam dunk!

Star student shows off her winning formula

The queen receives a warm welcome

She put the story in the **news**, and every word was **true**.

Everyone had a sea-riously good time!

Snail surprise

A ROYAL SUCCESS!

Written by Mermaid Mia

We had a great time yesterday
with Queen Marina here.
And as she left, she told us all:
"I'll come again next year!"

After that, **Mia** was **truthful**,
even when the news was **slow**.

The Mermail

SHELL SHOCK:
Snails spotted
in the canteen!

She'd **learned** that being **honest**
was the **only** way to **go**!

Daisy the Donut Fairy

the Donut Fairy

Tim Bugbird · Lara Ede

Once upon an island
in the **deep blue** sea,
lived a **mermaid** fairy family –
Daisy, Dolly, and Dee.

Days were filled with **fun**
as the **fairies** swam and *flew,*
but apart from making **donuts,**
there wasn't much to do!

Donut
Island

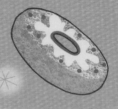

Their fairy wands made every kind —
hundreds by the hour!
But the donut mountains
grew and grew
'til there was no room in their tower.

So DAISY called a meeting of her fairy clan.
They put their heads together –
what they needed was a plan!

Daisy, Dee, and Dolly thought hard for **hours** and **hours**.
Finding **uses** for the *donuts*
used up all their **fairy powers!**

Wheels

The **first** idea was Dolly's —
it didn't work the way she wished:
the **wheels** looked
good enough to eat
but soon got very **squished!**

Earrings

This was Dee's **best** idea,
but she didn't think it through –
they were far **too big** to dangle,
and the ℱrosting
stuck like glue!

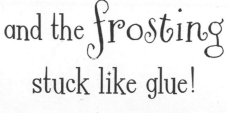

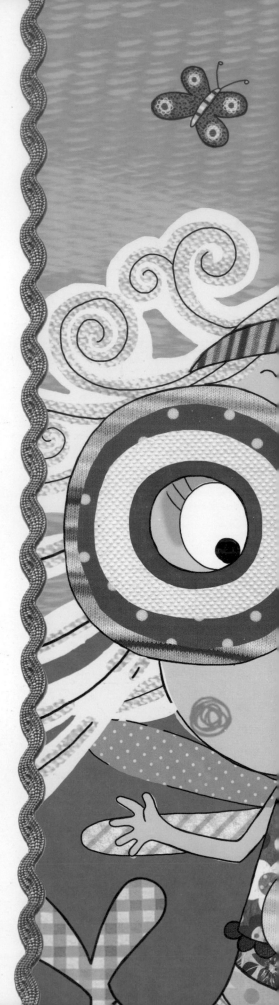

Sunglasses

The **third** idea was Daisy's.
At first it seemed quite good,
but **glasses** made from
donuts just don't
work the way they should!

It was **nothing**
less than **awful** –

there was **nothing**
left to **try**.

44

At least that's what
the **fairies** thought,
until a **pirate ship**
sailed by.

Pancake Pete was **all aboard**
with first mate Fearsome Fred,
but neither one could see the **rocks**
with the **pancakes** on their heads!

Overboard the pirates jumped

as their ship began to sink.

Uh-oh!
Crunch!

They splished and sploshed and sploshed and splashed and splished,

until they turned

bright pink!

Peering through the window
and thinking very fast,
Daisy said, "I think we have
a use for these at last!"

She took some donuts from the pile and threw them to the boat.
The pirates jumped inside the rings — they really helped them float!

The Pancake Pirates **bobbed** to shore,
their timbers all a-shiver.

Dee and Dolly felt quite scared,
and Daisy began to quiver.

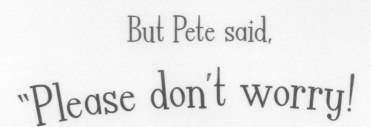

But Pete said,

"Please don't worry!

We're really
not **that** bad,

and sailing donut dinghies was the most fun we've ever had!"

The Pirates were so grateful and asked,

"What can we do?"

Daisy said,

"There's a job for us
in sea search and rescue!"

So the fairies and the pirates learned how to work together,
helping those in trouble at sea or lost in stormy weather.

Every day was an **adventure**,
hard work but full of **fun**,
and their **donuts**
had a use at last —
every single one!

So that's how DAISY'S donuts stopped the pirates sinking

and a mermaid fairy saved the day with true friends and quick thinking!

Meghan Sparkle
and the ROYAL BABY

Lara Ede · Rosie Greening

Once, in **Coral Kingdom**, an announcement came to say that a brand-new **royal baby** had been born that very day!

The King & Queen have a new baby called Bubble!

Almost all the mermaids thought the baby news was **great**.
But *Princess Meghan Sparkle* didn't **want** to celebrate.

She was baby Bubble's **sister**, but she found it all a **bore**.
From *Meghan's* point of view, her life was going **fine** before!

She could **play games** in the castle or **sing loudly** if she chose...

La - la - LAA!

...and always found a **quiet** place
to **read** a book or **doze**.

But now, the baby **screamed** so much,
it drove her up the wall,
and **smelled** so bad that *Meghan*
couldn't concentrate at all!

Wahhh h

Wahhhhhhhhh!

Calming sea sounds

One day, **Meghan** couldn't wait to read her book somewhere, when suddenly the sound of Bubble's **crying** filled the air.

Wahhhh!

Wahhhh!

Wahhhh!

So **Meghan** searched for somewhere **far away** from all the noise,

but every room was **smelly**...

full...

or **stuffed** with baby toys!

She slammed her book closed with a SMACK and shouted,
"IT'S NOT FAIR!

MER-TALES

Everyone's gone baby mad: I can't read ANYWHERE."

She sped outside and swam along
a winding path at speed,
until she found a silent spot:
the **PERFECT** place to read!

Meghan read her book for **hours**, as **happy** as a clam.

But **when** she tried to leave,
she cried . . .

"I don't know where I am!"

Clown Fish Corner

She swam out here so **quickly**,
she'd forgotten to keep track.
And now she simply **didn't know**
which path would take her back!

74

Just when she felt **lost at sea**,
the princess heard a cough.
The **mail-turtle** was swimming by,
dropping parcels off.

Seaweed Stables

Whale Way

"**Your Royal Highness!**" Turtle cried,
and gave a little bow.

"Can you help me?" Meghan asked.
"I've **lost my way** somehow!"

"I'll take you home," said Turtle,
"but I **must** drop off this mail."
"**That sounds fun!**" the mermaid said,
and joined him on his trail.

First, he had a parcel for the **clown fish** family,
who all lived **cramped together** in a small anemone.

"That looks **crowded**," Meghan thought,
and watched the clown fish play.
"I'm **lucky** I don't share a room
with Bubble every day."

Ooooooooh!

Ooooh!

A choir **singing** whale songs
was the next stop on their rounds.

But **Meghan** couldn't **understand**
the group's **unusual** sounds.

Turtle laughed:
"That's how they **speak**;
it just sounds odd to **you**."

Meghan thought of **Bubble's cries**...
could they mean something too?

They went to **Seaweed Stables** for their last delivery.
The little baby seahorses were racing with a

"wheeeeeee!"

This is fun!

I was born
to win!

Meghan and the turtle
watched the babies for a while.

"Maybe siblings **are** ok,"
thought Meghan with a smile.

With the packages delivered,
Meghan thought of what she'd seen.
And **suddenly** she realized
how **silly** she had been!

She said, "I **understand** now
that when all is said and done,
having someone **new** around
is going to be **fun!**"

The turtle guided **Meghan** back across the ocean floor,
and soon she heard a distant cry she **knew** she'd heard before.

"Thank you, Turtle!"
Meghan said.
"I recognize those sounds."
And then she followed Bubble's cries
into the castle grounds.

She rushed to **hug** the baby, feeling happy as can be.
"Hello Bubble," *Meghan* said. "I'm glad we're family."

After that, she didn't leave the royal baby's side,
and read her **favorite** books aloud
whenever Bubble cried.

So Meghan found some lovely friends, and as young Bubble grew,

she saw that life is wonderful when you are one of two!

Lola the Lollipop Fairy

Tim Bugbird · Lara Ede

Once upon a time
in a circus **big top**,
lived a fairy **family**,
the sisters Lollipop!

Every day at six o'clock,
come rain or shine or snow,
fairies came from far and wide
to see their famous show!

Lola was the one in charge

and Linda lifted weights.

Lulu juggled lollipops
and sometimes balanced plates!

Their act had been the same for years
and their tent was worn and old,
but every night they did their best
and all the seats were sold.

'Til one morning Lola woke;
she **yawned** and rubbed her eyes.
She looked outside and had a **shock** –
what a bad surprise!

Next door, where the grass had been,
the plants and trees and flowers,
there stood a brand-new theme park
with rides and slides and towers!

cat bed

The park became
the place to go,
where fairies met to play,
and no one
came to Lola's show.
She sighed, as if to say,
"The rides are so exciting,
we just cannot compete."
Lulu said, "Let's face it, friends,
I think we might be beat!"

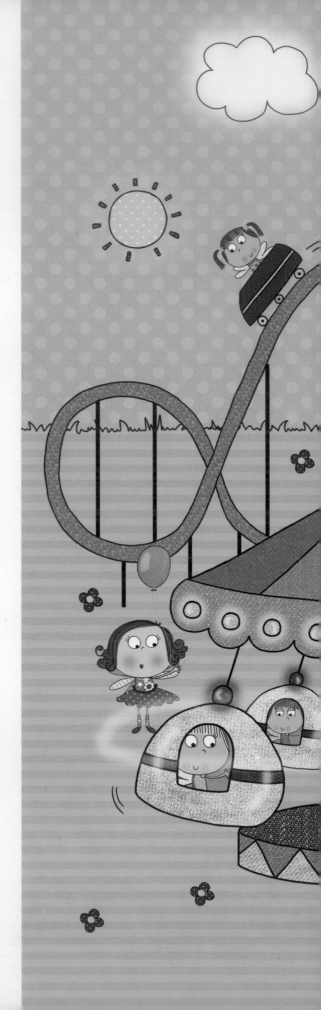

"So we'll just make our show better!"
Lola boldly cried.
"We'll do our best, so if we fail,
at least we'll know we tried!"

"Let's think of something super big,
a spectacular creation,
a show to make the fairies talk —
we'll be the new sensation!"

In a flash it came to Lola —
a plan to make them swoon.
Lola the Fairy Cannonball
would fly up to the moon!

So the fairies built a cannon
that was just the perfect size
to fire fearless Lola
from the circus to the skies!
They banged and bashed,
and clanged and clashed
until the job was done.
The work was hard,
the hours were long,
but they'd never had such fun!

The day for launching Lola
came around really fast.

Linda hollered, "Three, two, one!"
and, with a deafening BLAST,

Lola shot up into space
as the fairies waved and cheered.
And Lola thought, "What a lovely place,
I'm glad I volunteered!"

And when Lola finally landed, she cried:
"Oh my goodness, golly!
I thought the moon was made of cheese,
but it's a great big orange lolly!"

It certainly was the sweetest place
Lola had ever seen,
with lollipops of every kind
and mountains of whipped cream!

The air was
sweet as strawberries
and the sky was
pink and clear.
Lola flew back down to earth —
she'd had a new idea.

Her cannon show had been a blast,
but this plan was the ace.
They'd make their fairy fortunes
firing fairies into space!

And so the sisters got to work, they never seemed to stop.
Soon the moon trips made enough to buy a

new BIG TOP!

With a brand-new sparkly cannon,
glitter, and lights aglow,
very soon the stage was set
for their amazing circus show!

It was thrilling and exciting,
a full house every night.
The fairies saved the circus
thanks to Lola's daring flight!

So Lola, Linda, and Lulu made the perfect team.

By working hard, and not giving up, they lived their fairy dream!

Just NARWHAL

Lara Ede • Rosie Greening

Narwhal was a whale who thought
she had **no skills** at all.

She couldn't **cook**...

or knit...

or sing...

or even
catch a ball!

Meanwhile, all her **mermaid** friends
were skillful as can be.
If they tried out something **new**,
they did it **perfectly**.

"**Wow!**" thought Narwhal every day.
"There's nothing they can't do.
But I'm **just Narwhal**,
and I wish that I had **talent** too."

One morning, Star and Coral cried to **Narwhal** in distress:

"Our **art contest** has started, but everything's a **mess!**"

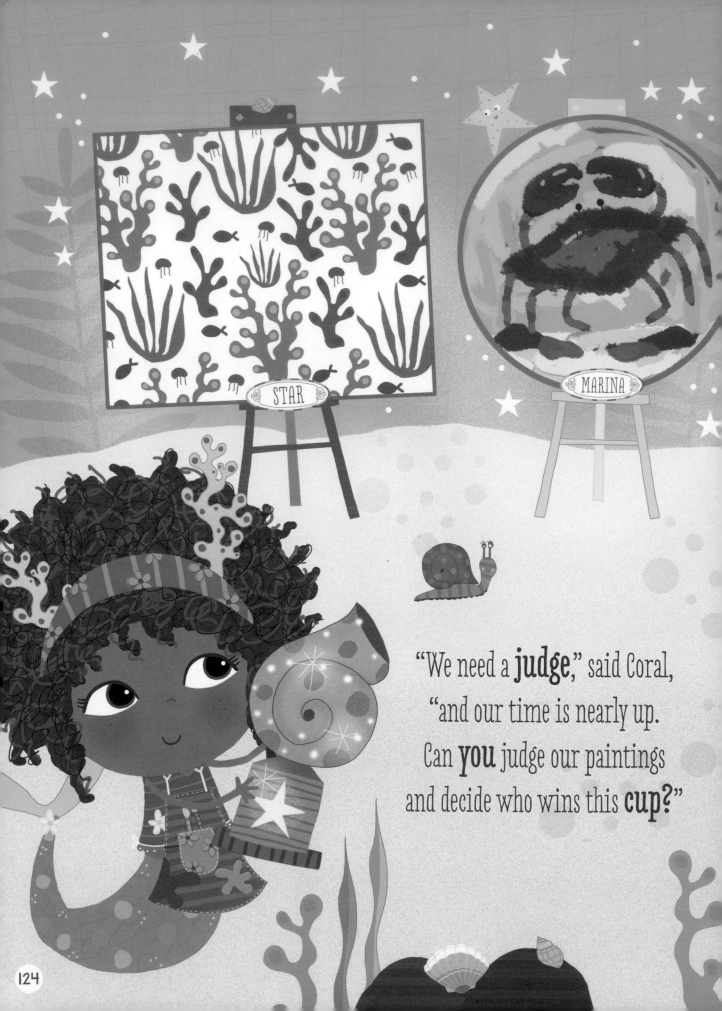

STAR

MARINA

"We need a **judge**," said Coral,
"and our time is nearly up.
Can **you** judge our paintings
and decide who wins this **cup?**"

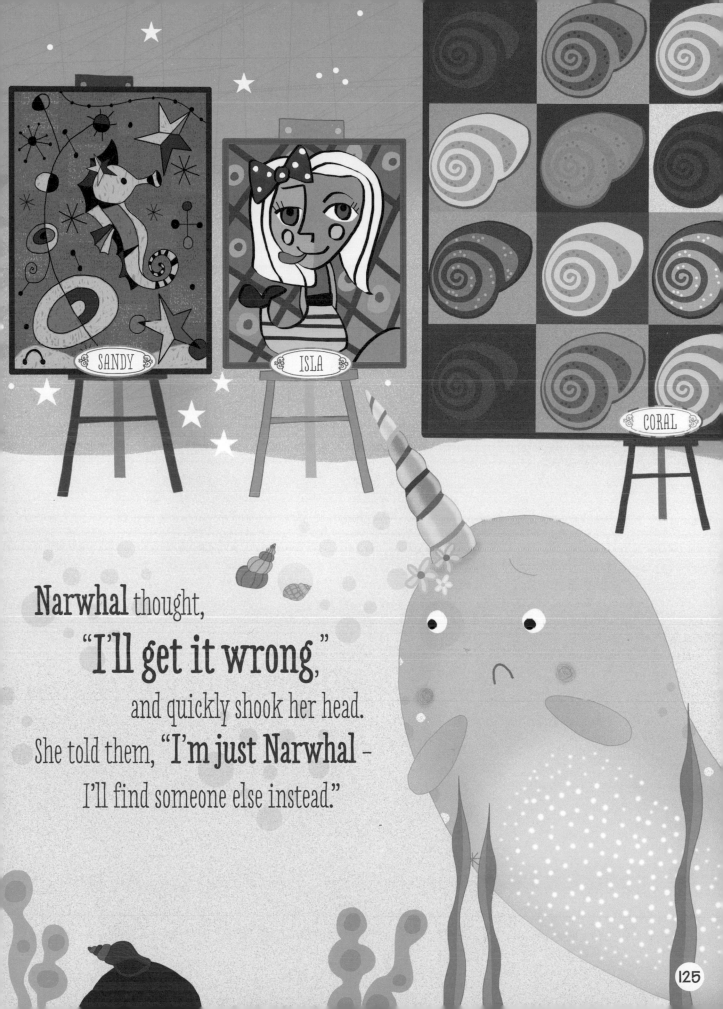

Narwhal thought,
"I'll get it wrong,"
and quickly shook her head.
She told them, "I'm just Narwhal –
I'll find someone else instead."

She asked **Cackle the Clown Fish**
to decide which art should win.

ISLA

"The prize goes to the

FUNNIEST!

said Cackle with a grin.

Narwhal thought,
  "That's not enough to win the special prize.
  But I'm **just Narwhal**, so I'll check
  with someone **big** and **wise**."

She found a **big blue whale** and asked,
"Which painting is the **best?**"

"The

BIGGEST!"

shouted Jumbo.
"**Forget** about the rest!"

"I'm not sure size is **everything**," said Narwhal quietly.
"But since I am **just Narwhal**,
I'll make sure **Shelly** agrees."

Shelly scuttled around the art, but judged them **selfishly**.
The shellfish said, "The **winner** is the one that features . . .

ME!"

MARINA

Narwhal looked around and thought,
"These choices **don't** seem fair.

ISLA

CORAL

MARINA

They **can't** judge on **one thing** alone:
there's **much** more to compare."

Narwhal swam to join her friends.
"I've let you down!" she cried.
"You need a **fair** and **honest** judge,
who sees how **hard** you tried."

The mermaids said, "If that's the case, then **YOU** should judge our art! To us, you're not '**just Narwhal**,' and we'd **love** you to take part."

Narwhal gave a
nervous smile and said,
"Okay, I'll try!"

And she wrote a list of **qualities**
to judge the paintings by.

Narwhal swam around the art,
and **studied** each with care.
She looked at **every** brush stroke
to make sure that she was **fair**.

- Colors ☑
- Theme ☑
- Brushstroke ☐
- Technique ☐
- Effort ☐
- Beauty ☐

ISLA

SANDY

At last she said, "Each piece of art
is **special** in its way.
But **ONE** checked every box for me . . .

Star wins first prize today!"

Star held up the shining cup
for **everyone** to see.
Then Coral rushed to Narwhal,
and she **hugged** her gratefully.

She said, "You are the **finest** judge
we could have ever found.
You're **fair** and **open-minded**...

...the most
JUST narwhal around!"

From that day on, **Narwhal** would judge
each contest she could find.

FINISH

And though she couldn't dance or sing, at last, she didn't **mind**.

She thought,

"My **skills** are hidden –
they're not **obvious** to see.
But just like all the **paintings**,

there is so much
more to me!"

Sparkle Town Fairies

Daphne the Diamond Fairy

and the Catwalk Catastrophe

Sarah Creese * Lara Ede

On **Sparkle Town's** main shopping street,
there stood a grand **boutique**,

Main Street

filled with **dresses**, hats, and shoes
so cute, and oh-so chic!

DIAMOND BOUTIQUE

Every **dress** was quite unique –
but one thing did not vary:
each stitch and style was made by hand
by **Daphne** the **Diamond Fairy**.

Diamonds
are always
in style.

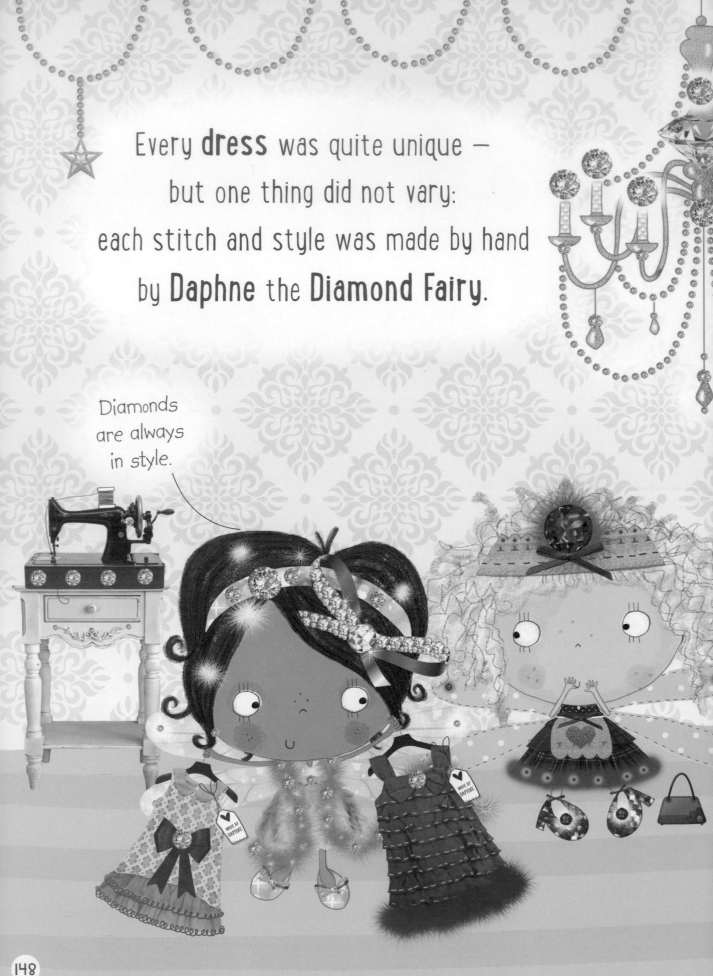

The fairies flocked from miles around
to buy each new design —
at times poor Daphne had to shout,
"Please, darlings, wait in line!"

Ooh,
I love it!

First she sketched

and next she cut,

then it was time
to **sew**

in every color imaginable.
And lastly, for **extra glow**...

she swished her special
sparkle wand,
and with a twinkling smile,

Perfect!

there appeared a
dazzling diamond —
her signature fairy style.

One morning Daphne left for work,
but as she turned the corner,

Flutter
Flutter

Main Street

a letter carried by **Fluttermail** unfurled itself before her.

You've got mail!

"*Dear Daphne,*"
it read, in fancy script.
"*We hereby invite you to sew*
six dresses
for the one, the only,
Queenie Quartz's
Fashion Show."

Entry by invitation only.
Designs judged by Queenie Quartz herself,
head of Top Fairy, Fairy Land's most successful
fashion store ever — no really, EVER.

Queenie Quartz

Flutter
Flutter

153

Filled with glee,
she **whizzed** to work
to start her dress collection.

"It has to be my best," she said
"To win I need perfection."

All day and night
she **waved** her wand
but nothing seemed
quite right.

Then, by chance,
she tripped
and swished!

Swish!
Swoosh!

Swoo-oops!

From her wand
came a **wondrous sight**...

A shower of **glittering diamonds**,
covering each and every dress.

Daphne blinked from the diamonds' dazzle.
This look was **THE ONE** to impress!

The next day, Daphne's friends arrived
to be fitted for the show.
Daphne revealed her new designs
and they **gasped** at the glamorous glow.

You look
dazzling.

No, you look
dazzling.

But seeing her friends look so sublime,
Daphne's thoughts turned jealous and sour.
"Why should **they** be the ones to shine
and steal my finest hour?"

Daphne, these are
spurkletastic!

Hmm.

And in a whirl
she frowned,
then **snapped**,
"I'm afraid this
just won't do.
My **creations**
are far too good –
they'll look
better on **ME**
than you."

I'll wear ALL of them.

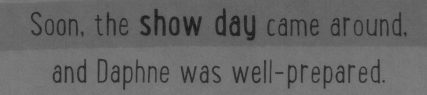

Soon, the **show day** came around,
and Daphne was well-prepared.

Her friends, meanwhile, sat at the back
(they were hurt, but they still cared).

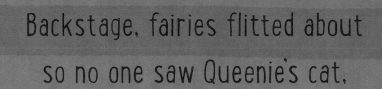

Backstage, fairies flitted about
so no one saw Queenie's cat,

who chased a feathery bird

(well, a dress)

causing a **catastrophe** that...

knocked a pole,

Clunk

made a rug unroll

Slip

Slide

and toppled a
teetering tower,

which broke
a big switch –

ON →

a disastrous glitch –

Woah!

AND...

165

TURNED OFF ALL THE POWER!

In the dark, the fairies flapped,
but Daphne had an **idea**.
By wand-light, something caught her eye
and made the **answer** clear.

"I can't do this alone," she thought,
and **rushed** to find her friends.
"I know now I was wrong," she said.
"Can we ever make amends?
I'm **sorry** for being selfish;
it was mean and unfair, too."
The fairies **smiled**, then **hugged** their friend
and said, "What can we do?"

Here's
the plan...

Wowzer!

She gave each friend a **diamond dress**,
then told them where to go.
"Fairies at the ready," she cried,
"it's time to save this **show!**"

Who needs lights!

Daphne swooshed her **diamond wand** —
up high, then left to right.
She bounced a beam from dress to dress,
filling the room with **LIGHT!**

The show was such a great success
that Queenie had to say,

"Dear Daphne, will you come each year
to be our **light display?**"

170

And though the fairies' dresses
sparkled beyond compare,
the thing that **sparkled** most of all
was the **friendship** that they **shared!**

Molly the Muffin Fairy

Tim Bugbird · Lara Ede

Molly the Muffin Fairy
was famous in Fairyland
for making perfect muffins –
some small and some quite grand.

Each one was baked 'til **spongy**,
golden, soft, and sweet.
Her wand put in big **blueberries**
to make the *treats* complete!

The blueberries came in boxes, delivered by **Mel** and **Kerri**, her two **best friends**, who drove a truck shaped like a **giant berry!**

But then one day when **baking**,
Molly's temper began to **fray**;
her **muffins** had no softness —
she was having a **bad** bake day!

Her baking got **no better**,

and soon **Molly's** fairy home

was full of **rubbery muffins**

with tops as hard as **stone!**

Molly was not happy.
The baking was making her MAD!
She fussed and fumed and finally flipped!
What she did was really bad . . .

She grabbed a tray of muffins
and threw them to the floor,
then took a muffin in her hand
and hurled it out the door!

The muffin hit her trampoline and **bounced** up in the air.

The strangest scene there's *ever* been
followed on from there . . .

It bounced and bumped
and pinged and ponged,
flying to and fro,
startling a squirrel,
who scampered and woke
a porcupine down below!

Up with a **start**, the porcupine **ran**
to find a **safe place** to hide.
But he **poked** the edge of **Molly's** pool —
his **spikes** making **holes** in the side!

Water gushed out from the holes,
flooding the road all around.

Then Mel and Kerri's truck arrived, but **how** would they cross the **wet** ground?

Berry Truck

Molly cried, "It's all a mess!"
Mel said, "Oh, stop whining!
Those muffins of yours could help us —
every cloud has a silver lining!"

"Maybe they could make a **path**. Just try and see."
So **Molly** laid the **muffins** down . . .
and the truck crossed **easily!**

Berry Truck

Blueberries

Blueberries

Then, before the **fairies'** eyes,
the **muffins** began to expand.
Soaking up water, they became
the **biggest** in Fairyland!

"The muffins feel soft!" cried Molly.
"Don't eat them, though; they're not clean!

But squashed together, I think they'll make . . ."

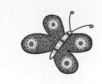

"...the best-ever trampoline!"